EXPLORE TITANIC

BREATHTAKING NEW PICTURES, RECREATED WITH DIGITAL TECHNOLOGY

Peter Chrisp

With illustrations by
Somchith Vongprachanh

CARLTON

This is a Carlton book

Text and artwork copyright
© 2011 Carlton Books Limited
Design copyright
© 2011 Carlton Books Limited

Original concept: *Darren Jordan*
Project Editor: *Paul Virr*
Written by: *Peter Chrisp*
Creative Director: *Darren Jordan*
Illustrator: *Somchith Vongprachanh*
Designer: *Danny Baldwin*
Cover Design: *Ceri Hurst*
Picture Research: *Steve Behan*
Additional photography: *Karl Adamson*
Production: *Kate Pimm*

Published in 2011 by Carlton Books Limited, an imprint of the Carlton Publishing Group,
20 Mortimer Street, London, W1T 3JW.

2 4 6 8 10 9 7 5 3 1

A catalogue record for this book is available from the British Library.

ISBN: 978-1-84732-883-0

Printed in South China.

Explore Titanic

No other ship has captured the imagination as powerfully as *Titanic*, yet just a handful of black-and-white photographs remain to give us an idea of how the ship really looked – until now.

We have gone back to the original plans to digitally recreate *Titanic* using ultra-real 3D graphics. Finally, you can see *Titanic* as she was, in colour and in all her glory. These amazing new views of *Titanic* are so real that you won't believe your eyes!

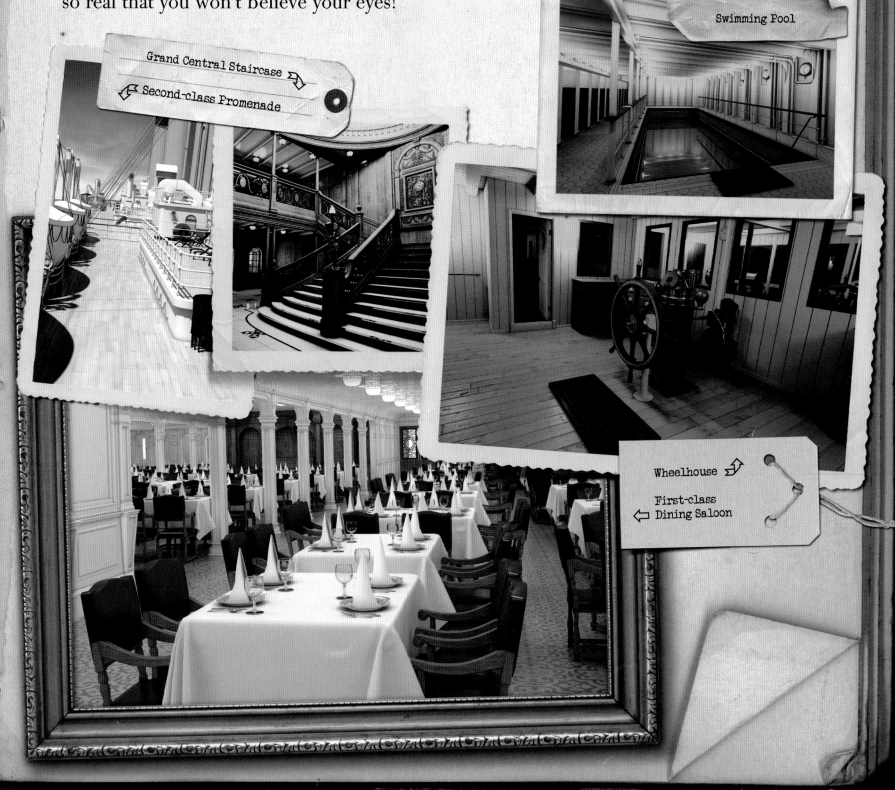

Grand Central Staircase

Second-class Promenade

Swimming Pool

Wheelhouse

First-class Dining Saloon

THE BIG IDEA

The early 1900s were the golden age of the ocean liner, with more than a million people emigrating from Europe to the US each year. Two British shipping companies competed for passengers who wished to cross the Atlantic: White Star and Cunard.

R.M.S. "MAURETANIA."

RIVALS FOR THE RIBAND

The liner that made the fastest Atlantic crossing was allowed to fly a long blue banner known as the Blue Riband from the mast. In 1907, Cunard beat White Star to the prize with the *Mauretania* and kept it for 22 years.

At its launch, RMS *Mauretania* was the fastest ship in the world. With a top speed of about 26 knots (48km/h), it could cross the Atlantic in a week.

BIGGER AND BETTER

Cunard's success worried James Bruce Ismay, the Managing Director of White Star, and his ship-building partner, Lord William Pirrie. In 1907, they came up with a plan to give them the edge over Cunard. White Star would build three huge liners, the world's largest passenger ships, each one-and-a-half times larger than Cunard's *Mauretania*.

LORD WILLIAM PIRRIE

JAMES BRUCE ISMAY

SAILING IN STYLE

White Star's new liners wouldn't be as fast as the *Mauretania*, but they would earn more money by carrying more passengers. They would also attract the richest customers by being incredibly luxurious. The design and the furniture would be so grand that passengers might think they were in a posh hotel rather than on board a ship.

It took several months to design *Titanic*, here in the Harland and Wolff drawing office.

In their advertising, White Star boasted about the sheer size of the first two new ships, *Olympic* and *Titanic*.

MAKING PLANS

The new ships would be built in Belfast by Lord Pirrie's company, Harland and Wolff. Thomas Andrews, Pirrie's nephew, was head of its design department. Andrews and his team now set about designing the largest ships ever to be built. They made thousands of detailed plans, all drawn by hand. Andrews was very proud of their work and thought that *Titanic* was the perfect ship.

Watertight compartments

(For Description, see Page 802.)

UNSINKABLE?

For safety, the designers divided the lower part of each ship into 16 watertight compartments. In an emergency, these compartments would be sealed off by electrically operated doors. The ship could then stay afloat – as long as no more than two compartments were flooded.

> "*This ship is as nearly perfect as human brains can make her.*"
>
> **Thomas Andrews to a passenger on the *Titanic*.**

THOMAS ANDREWS

BUILDING TITANIC

With the plans complete, the massive task of building the *Titanic* and her sister ships, *Olympic* and *Britannic*, began. It took the Harland and Wolff shipyards two years to build them.

BUILT IN BELFAST

Harland and Wolff was the world's leading shipbuilding company. Based in Belfast, Ireland, it used the latest technology and was known for getting work done on time and on budget.

HARLAND & WOLFF, LIMITED.

Builders of the "OLYMPIC" and "TITANIC," the largest steamers in the World, 45,000 tons each.

BELFAST WORKS.

This advertisement for Harland and Wolff shows the huge scale of the shipyards where *Titanic* was built.

A TITANIC TEAM

It took a workforce of about 3,000 men and boys to build *Titanic*. It was dangerous work – more than 450 of them were injured and 17 died during construction.

FIRST STEPS

Before work could begin, two new slipways were built between a massive steel framework called a gantry. The gantry was used for moveable cranes.

WORK BEGINS

The first part of the ship to be built was the keel – the metal backbone of the ship. The keel was laid down on 31 March 1909 and stretched for 269m – longer than two football pitches.

SHIP SHAPE

Along the keel, a series of curved metal ribs called frames were added. These gave *Titanic* its shape. The metal plates that made up the outer shell of the ship would later be attached to the frames.

A riveter using a hydraulic riveting machine. It took five years of on-the-job training to become a skilled riveter.

WATERTIGHT

The next job was to attach sheets of steel to the outside of the ship to make a watertight hull. The outer skin of *Titanic* was made of steel plates, 2.5cm thick. These hull plates were held in place with iron or steel rivets.

FIXING THE PLATES

At the bows and stern of *Titanic*, all the rivets were fixed by hand by a manual riveting team of three men and two boys. In the central section of the ship, where there was more room, bulky new riveting machines could be used.

Over 3 million rivets were used. The workers were paid for each rivet fitted, so they worked as quickly as they could!

At the stern, the workers fitted the central propeller and two side propellers that would drive the ship along.

RIVETING

Riveting was a highly skilled job. Each rivet was heated in a furnace until it was red hot, then it was placed in a hole on the hull plate and the ends were hammered flat.

READY TO SAIL

Soon after noon, on 31 May 1911, *Titanic* was launched. A crowd of 100,000 cheered as the ship took just over a minute to slide down the slipway into the water.

LAUNCH DAY
At its launch, *Titanic* was mostly an empty shell, yet she still weighed around 26,000 tonnes – making her the heaviest object ever moved by people. She was pushed down the greased slipway with a machine operated by the shipyard manager, Charles Payne.

Launch

OF

White Star Royal Mail Triple-Screw Steamer

"TITANIC"

At BELFAST,

Wednesday, 31st May, 1911, at 12-15 p.m.

Admit Bearer.

The White Star Line sold tickets to watch the launch of *Titanic*. All the money raised went to charity.

One of *Titanic*'s huge boilers being lifted into the empty shell of the ship, which had yet to be fitted with its four funnels.

FIXTURES AND FITTINGS
After the launch, *Titanic* was towed to the deepwater outfitting wharf, where work continued on her for more than ten months. Here the engines, funnels and the luxurious interiors were fitted.

TEST DRIVE
Before she could carry passengers, *Titanic* had to pass a series of tests called sea trials. On 2 April 1912, she was towed to the open waters of Belfast Lough where she sailed under her own power for the first time.

SEAWORTHY
The ship made circles at various speeds. In an emergency-stop test it took her three minutes and 15 seconds to come to a halt and she covered 777m. This was satisfactory for such a large vessel and *Titanic* was officially declared seaworthy.

Pulled by five tugs, *Titanic* enters Belfast Lough for her sea trials.

CAPTAIN E. J. SMITH

SAILING TO SOUTHAMPTON

Immediately after passing her sea trials, *Titanic* set sail for Southampton, with a small crew under the command of Captain E. J. Smith. He was the most experienced captain of the White Star Line and had previously been captain of *Titanic*'s sister ship, the *Olympic*.

"In forty years at sea … I never saw a wreck and never have been wrecked." **Captain E. J. Smith**

Before departure, the ship's whistles sounded three blasts that could be heard across the city.

FINISHING TOUCHES

At midnight on 3 April 1912, *Titanic* reached Southampton. Over the next week, 724 more crew members joined the ship and vast quantities of stores were loaded. The final touches were also made to the ship's interior decoration, as carpets were laid and curtains hung.

TAKING ON PASSENGERS

On the morning of Wednesday 10 April, about 1,000 passengers came aboard and were shown to their cabins. Finally, at noon, *Titanic* set off on her first voyage, bound for France, Ireland and America.

Titanic, moored in Southampton, where a massive new dock had been built for the huge White Star liners.

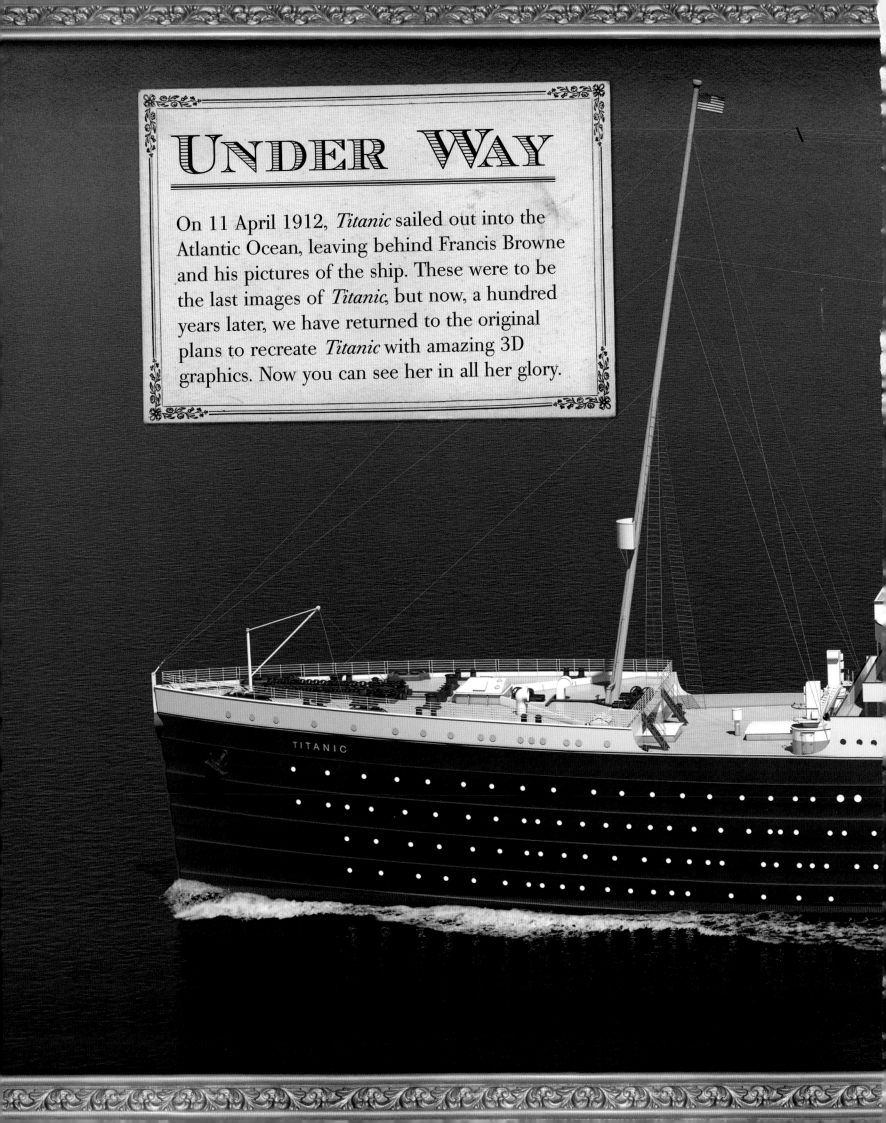

UNDER WAY

On 11 April 1912, *Titanic* sailed out into the Atlantic Ocean, leaving behind Francis Browne and his pictures of the ship. These were to be the last images of *Titanic*, but now, a hundred years later, we have returned to the original plans to recreate *Titanic* with amazing 3D graphics. Now you can see her in all her glory.

The Voyage Begins

Titanic made two short stops to take aboard more passengers, at Cherbourg in France and Queenstown in Ireland. On 11 April, she finally set sail for New York, carrying 1,324 passengers and 899 crew.

A FLOATING POST OFFICE

At each stop, the ship also picked up sacks of mail – more than 4,500 sacks holding some 400,000 letters. These, plus all the mail sent by the passengers, would be sorted during the voyage by the ship's five postal clerks.

These mailbags, carried aboard in Queenstown, were filled with letters from Irish people to relatives who had emigrated to the US.

Triple-Screw R.M.S.
"OLYMPIC" and "TITANIC,"
46,000 Tons each.
The Largest Steamers
in the World.

WHITE STAR LINE

ROYAL MAIL SHIP

The ship's full title was RMS *Titanic*, the initials RMS standing for Royal Mail Ship. Royal Mail Ships had to be fast and reliable. A ship that delivered the post late would be fined and could lose its official RMS title.

In Queenstown, a passenger named Robert Phillips sent this postcard to a friend, saying, 'We are all right up to now and having a jolly time.'

FAREWELL TO IRELAND

On the Queenstown harbour front, 123 Irish passengers said tearful farewells to relatives and joined the ship. All but ten had third-class tickets. They were mostly poor young men and women from the countryside, hoping to find a better life in America.

WHITE STAR LINE AMERICAN LINE.

Irish passengers wait on the White Star wharf in Queenstown (now Cobh) in Ireland, photographed from *Titanic* by Francis Browne before he left the ship.

RMS *Titanic* under way in the Atlantic Ocean

As Titanic sails past, you can see two flags fluttering from the masts.
The US Stars and Stripes, on the forward mast, showed her destination.
On the rear mast, she flew the emblem of the White Star Line.

RMS *TITANIC*: FACTS AND FIGURES

Length: 269.1m
Width: 28.2m
Height, from the keel to top of funnels: 53.3m
Height, from the water line to the top deck: 18m
Number of decks: 10
Top speed: 23 knots (43km/h)
Passengers: 2,603 maximum
Crew: 944 maximum
Boilers: 29
Boiler furnaces: 162
Engines: 3
Lifeboats: 20 (including four collapsible lifeboats)

At sea, the lookouts discovered that their binoculars had gone missing, so they would have to rely on the naked eye alone.

FRANCIS BROWNE

ONE LAST PICTURE

Francis Browne, a student priest and a keen amateur photographer, left *Titanic* in Queenstown with his camera and dozens of photographic plates. His pictures are the only visual record of the ship's voyage.

Francis Browne took one of the last pictures of *Titanic*, as she left Ireland, her stern crowded with third-class passengers.

FULL STEAM AHEAD

FURNACE Nº 7

Everything on *Titanic* was driven by steam power, from the ship's propellers to the lights, heating and the lifts. Steam was provided by 29 massive boilers, heated by 162 coal-burning furnaces.

STEAM POWER

The boilers produced steam, which was fed to three massive engines, each turning one of the ship's propellers. In the rear of the ship, the steam powered four smaller engines to generate electricity for the whole ship.

The engines that drove the propellers were as tall as a three-storey house.

FEEDING THE FURNACES

Below decks, teams of stokers shovelled coal into the furnaces that heated the boilers. They also raked out about 100 tonnes of ash a day. The work was hot and dangerous. Stokers wore clogs to protect their feet from burning coals.

DIRTY WORK

In the bunkers above and between the boilers, 'trimmers' kept the coal level and shovelled it down chutes to the stokers below. It was a filthy job and they wore wet rags over their faces to keep out the coal dust.

Titanic's 176 stokers and 73 trimmers were usually covered in black coal dust, so they were nicknamed the 'black gang'.

BOILER ROOM: ORLOP DECK
You are standing in one of the six boiler rooms on Titanic.
Each of these rooms spanned the width of the ship and had
four or five boilers arranged side by side.

WELCOME ABOARD

Titanic was designed to be the most luxurious ship in the world, with lavish interiors to rival the grand hotels. As a first-class passenger, you would travel in style, right from the moment you caught the special first-class boat train to Southampton.

A FIRST-CLASS WELCOME

The ship carried 325 first-class passengers, including several US millionaires. Many travelled with servants, maids, nurses and chauffeurs. Their staterooms, some with their own private decks, were on the ship's upper levels, far from the noise of the engines. As they walked down the Grand Central Staircase, they would have felt as if they had just arrived for a stay in an expensive hotel.

First-class passengers walk up the gangplank to the Boat Deck as they board *Titanic* in Southampton.

STEWARDS AND STEWARDESSES

Passengers were looked after by an army of stewards and stewardesses, each wearing a numbered badge. They took care of all the daily needs of passengers: helping them dress, cleaning their rooms, bringing drinks, walking their dogs and even comforting them if they felt seasick.

Stewards wore smart white jackets that made them easy to recognise. They could be called at any time with an electric bell

A DECK: GRAND CENTRAL STAIRCASE
You are standing before the Grand Central Staircase in first class. This impressive sweep of stairs greeted first-class passengers as they came down from the Boat Deck into the luxurious interior of the ship.

TRAVELLING FIRST CLASS

Titanic had 39 first-class suites on decks B and C, decorated in the styles of different historical periods. The suites included bedrooms, bathrooms, toilets, elegant lounges and extra rooms for servants.

UPPER CLASS

The suites and individual first-class cabins were all on the upper levels, far from the noise of the engines and within easy reach of the promenade deck. They were central, too, so first-class passengers didn't have far to walk to the Grand Central Staircase or the elevators.

This recreation of a first-class cabin from a museum shows how luxurious *Titanic's* cabins would have looked.

EVERY CONVENIENCE

An added luxury for the wealthiest passengers was a first-class cabin with its own private bathroom. These had hot and cold water, plus a modern shower spray. Other passengers had to use the public baths.

This White Star publicity picture shows one of the first-class bathrooms.

JOHN JACOB ASTOR

The richest passenger was John Jacob Astor, a millionaire who was returning to the US with his new wife. They travelled with a valet, a maid, a nurse, and a pet dog called Kitty, and occupied first-class cabins C62-4.

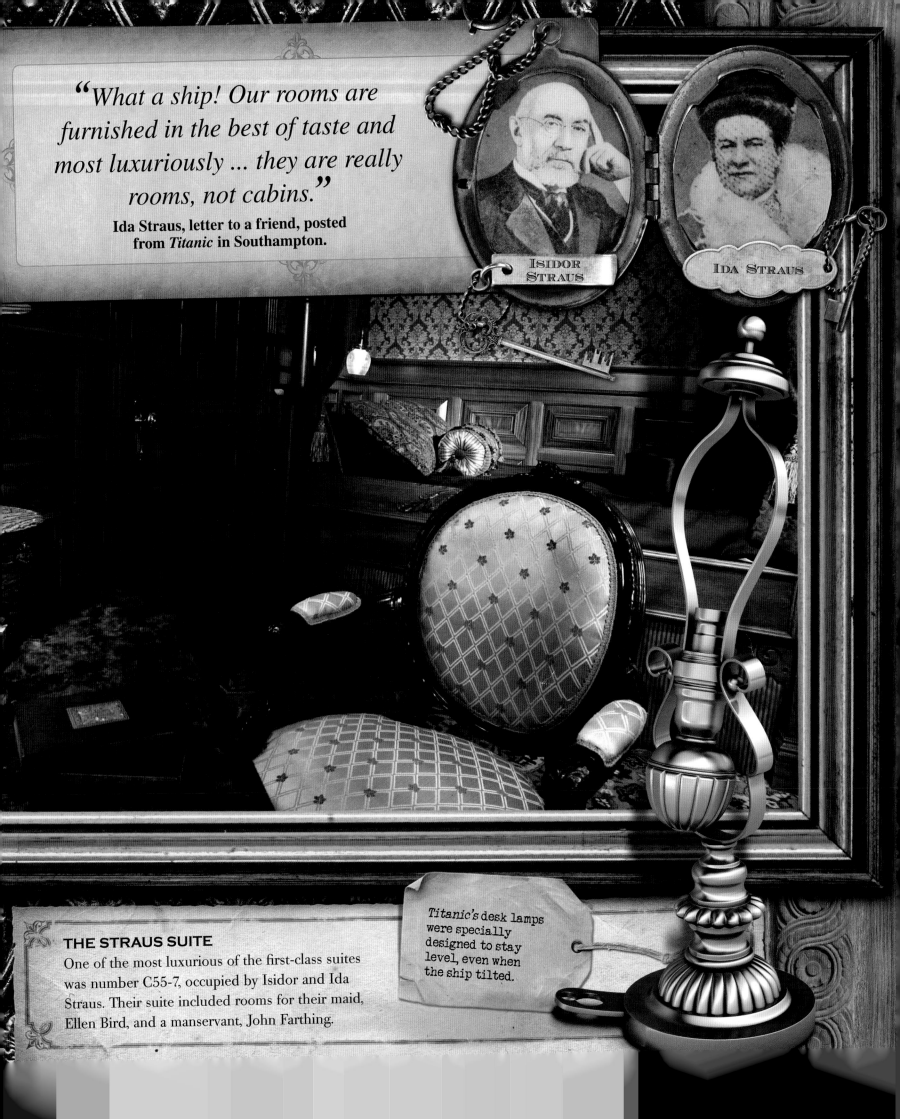

> *"What a ship! Our rooms are furnished in the best of taste and most luxuriously ... they are really rooms, not cabins."*
>
> **Ida Straus, letter to a friend, posted from *Titanic* in Southampton.**

ISIDOR STRAUS

IDA STRAUS

THE STRAUS SUITE

One of the most luxurious of the first-class suites was number C55-7, occupied by Isidor and Ida Straus. Their suite included rooms for their maid, Ellen Bird, and a manservant, John Farthing.

Titanic's desk lamps were specially designed to stay level, even when the ship tilted.

OUT AND ABOUT

First-class passengers found plenty to do onboard. They could walk on the promenade deck or use the gymnasium, squash court and swimming pool. To relax, they could visit the Turkish bath or one of the cafés.

> "*I had a long promenade and a doze for an hour up to five o'clock. The band played in the afternoon for tea, but I savour a coffee in the Verandah café with bread and butter.*"
>
> **Adolphe Saafeld, first-class passenger.**

A Deck: Covered First-class Promenade
You are standing in the covered first-class promenade area. It stretched for 152m, more than the length of six tennis courts, so there was plenty of space to stroll.

A WALK ON DECK

The promenade deck reserved for the use of first-class passengers was a very lively place. Passengers would chat as they walked around or sat in deckchairs enjoying the sea air. It was sheltered from rain and bad weather by the Boat Deck above.

Teak deckchairs, known as steamer chairs, could be reserved before the voyage began or hired while the ship was at sea.

LOUNGING ABOUT

For snacking between meals, there were three first-class cafés: the Verandah, the Palm Court and the Café Parisien. Families with children tended to choose the Verandah Café, while fashionable young people preferred the stylish Café Parisien.

The Café Parisien was like a fashionable Paris café, with the added advantage of a sea view through large picture windows.

The decorated china cups that first-class passengers sipped their tea from were specially made for *Titanic*.

KEEPING FIT

The gymnasium was up on the Boat Deck and had the latest equipment, including rowing and cycling machines, plus an electric camel and two electric horses! A fitness instructor, like a personal trainer, was on hand to help passengers use the machines.

Thomas McCawley, *Titanic's* fitness instructor, demonstrates how to use the rowing machine.

A richly carved screen over the portholes cast patterns of light on the walls to create an exotic atmosphere.

TURKISH BATH

The Turkish bath was decorated with colourful blue and green tiles and Arabic-style lamps. It had a steam room, hot and cool rooms, and even an electric bath – an early version of a sunbed where passengers could get a tan.

A DIP IN THE POOL

On the middle deck of *Titanic*, next to the Turkish bath, there was a swimming pool for the first-class passengers. This was one of the first swimming pools to be installed on an ocean liner.

DIVE IN

Visitors to the Turkish bath, hot from the sauna and steam room, would cool down with a refreshing plunge in the pool. Others went straight to the pool to swim lengths, working up an appetite for their next big meal.

A White Star publicity painting of the pool shows bathers in blue knitted swimsuits.

Alongside the pool were a row of changing rooms and showers.

" ... met the professional racquet player in a half-hour's warming up for a swim in the six foot deep tank of saltwater heated to a refreshing temperature."

Colonel Archibald Gracie, first-class passenger.

COLONEL ARCHIBALD GRACIE

F Deck: The Swimming Pool

You are standing by the swimming pool, which was 9.1m long, 4.3m wide and 1.8m deep. It was filled with sea water, warmed to room temperature by the ship's boilers. When the ship was moving, the pool's surface rippled with vibrations.

DINNER IS SERVED

For the first-class passengers, dinner on *Titanic* was a grand occasion. They dressed elegantly for dinner, with the men all wearing identical black tailcoats and white bow ties. The ladies wore expensive gowns and their finest jewellery.

This first-class menu shows the wide variety of dishes available for dinner.

R.M.S. TITANIC.

APRIL 10, 1912.

HORS D'ŒUVRE VARIÈS

CONSOMMÉ RÉJANE   CRÉME REINE MARGOT

TURBOT, SAUCE HOMARD
WHITEBAIT

MUTTON CUTLETS & GREEN PEAS
SUPRÉME OF CHICKEN À LA STANLEY

SIRLION OF BEEF, CHÂTEAU POTATOES
ROAST DUCKLING, APPLE SAUCE
FILLET OF VEAL & BRAISED HAM

CAULIFLOWER   SPINACH
BOILED RICE
BOVIN & BOILED NEW POTATOES

PLOVER ON TOAST & CR...
SALAD

PUDDING SANS...
CHARLOTTE CO...
GRANVIL...

FRENCH ICE...

Titanic carried 44,000 pieces of cutlery, 29,000 glasses and 57,600 plates and bowls.

DINNER TIME!
Before dinner, people gathered in the First-class Reception Room. They waited until the serving of dinner was announced by the ship's bugler, P.W. Fletcher, who played a tune called the 'Roast Beef of Old England'.

THE FINEST FOOD
Dinner had up to eleven courses, each served with a different wine. The French-style dishes were as good as those served in the best restaurants. Passengers could enjoy everything from a first course of oysters through to a dessert of French ice cream.

TABLE MANNERS
Dinner could last several hours and followed strict rules. Different plates, glasses and cutlery were used for each course, many decorated with the White Star emblem.

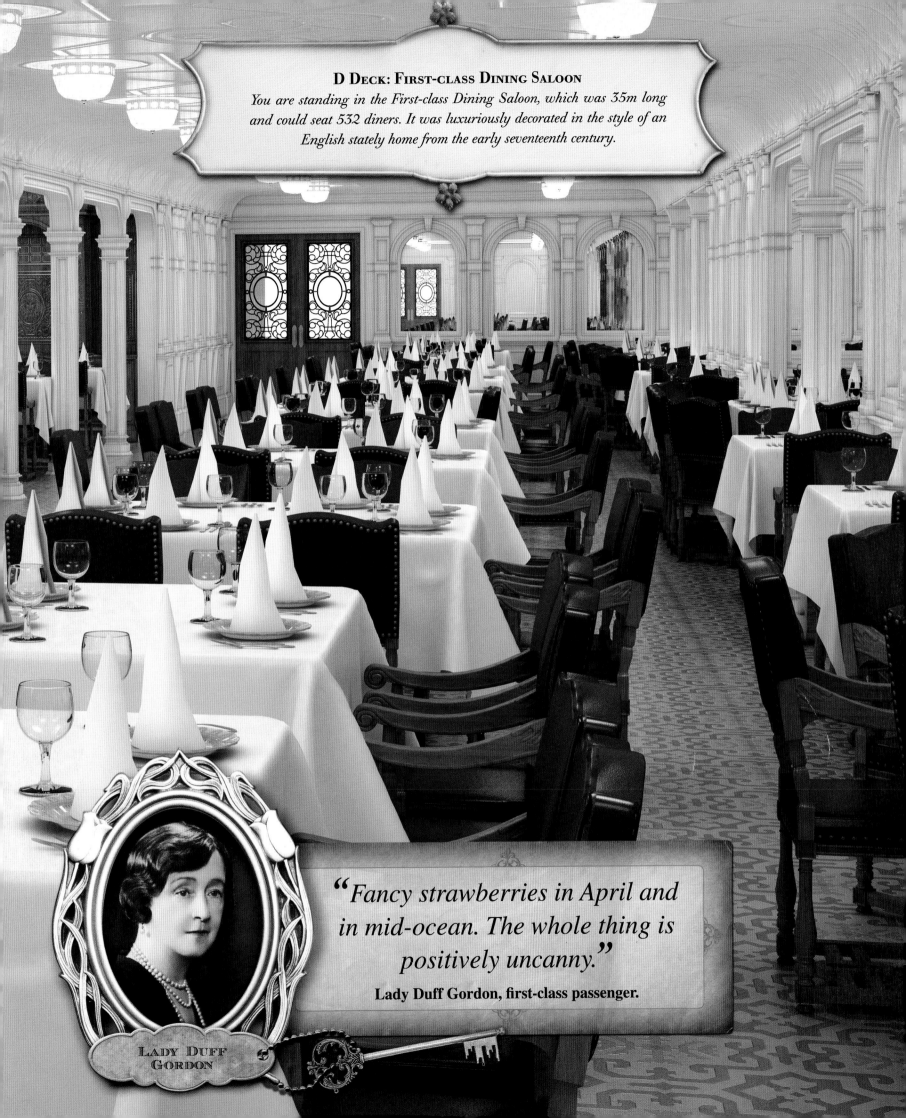

D Deck: First-class Dining Saloon

You are standing in the First-class Dining Saloon, which was 35m long and could seat 532 diners. It was luxuriously decorated in the style of an English stately home from the early seventeenth century.

> *"Fancy strawberries in April and in mid-ocean. The whole thing is positively uncanny."*
>
> **Lady Duff Gordon, first-class passenger.**

LADY DUFF GORDON

SECOND CLASS

Titanic's 285 second-class passengers were delighted with their cabins. They were in fact as luxurious as first class on many other ships.

A DIFFERENT CLASS

Second-class passengers were also impressed by the high quality meals served in the second-class saloon, where a pianist played as they ate. In those days, men and women usually separated after dinner. The men went off to the smoking room, while women went to the library or lounge.

COSY CABINS

The cabins were small, but comfortable, with up to four bunk beds, screened by curtains. There was a mahogany cabinet with a mirror, washbasin and tap for cold water. Passengers could ask their steward to bring a jug of hot water.

Second-class passengers stroll on their own section of the Boat Deck, with folded deckchairs to the right.

A White Star Line publicity picture shows a two-person second-class cabin, complete with a comfortable sofa to relax on.

BOAT DECK: SECOND-CLASS PROMENADE

You are standing in the second-class promenade area, which was in the rear part of the Boat Deck. The deck in front is divided into other promenade areas: for the engineers, first-class passengers and officers.

"The ship is like a palace ... my cabin has hot and cold water, a very comfy-looking bed and plenty of room."

Laurence Beesley, a teacher travelling to the US on holiday.

LAURENCE BEESLEY

In Steerage

Steerage was another name for third class. *Titanic* carried 706 third-class passengers. They came from more than 30 different countries, all hoping to find a new and better life in the US.

A FUTURE IN AMERICA

The third-class passengers included 104 Swedes. They had already made a long journey across the North Sea to Hull and then by train to Southampton. Among them was Carl Asplund, a 40-year-old farm labourer, travelling with his wife and five children. He was sure that the US would offer more opportunities than Sweden.

> *"California wants people like you. Now is your time to come here."*
>
> **Carl Asplund's notebook.**

Carl Asplund carried this notebook, in which he had carefully copied out an advert inviting settlers to move to California.

In Queenstown, Ireland, a US doctor inspects the eyes of Irish steerage passengers for symptoms of trachoma.

HEALTH CHECKS

Steerage passengers had to pass through strict health checks to be cleared for entry into the US. Before they could even board *Titanic*, they were checked for infectious diseases, such as trachoma, a disease causing blindness.

THIRD-CLASS CABINS

Third-class cabins were on the lower decks, towards the bows and the stern and closer to the noise of the engines. Although small, they were clean and modern, with electric light and heating and a washbasin, filled with cold water from a cistern.

The third-class dining rooms had individual chairs instead of the benches found on most other ships.

A third-class cabin, with two bunk beds. These had blankets and pillows stuffed with feathers, but no sheets.

ENTERTAINMENT

The ship had a third-class General Room for families and a smoking room with a bar for the men. Every evening, the passengers gathered in the General Room to play music, sing, dance and talk excitedly about their future in the US.

The General Room had white painted walls, decorated with colourful White Star Line posters of ships and their destinations.

FOOD WITHOUT FRILLS

There were two third-class dining rooms, with white enamelled walls. There was room for 473 people, so the passengers ate in two sittings. Meals, such as corned beef with boiled potatoes, were simple but filling. Fruit and freshly baked bread were also served with every meal.

The crockery in third-class was simple, but everything was decorated with the White Star Line emblem.

DISASTER STRIKES

On the evening of Sunday 14 April, *Titanic* was heading west, at slightly below top speed. There had been iceberg warnings, but Captain Smith didn't give the order to slow down.

SOUNDING THE ALARM

At 11.40pm, Frederick Fleet, a lookout in the crow's nest, saw a dark object in front of the ship. He rang his warning bell and telephoned the bridge, saying 'Iceberg, right ahead!'

The bell in *Titanic's* crow's nest was rung three times – the signal for danger right ahead.

TURNING THE SHIP

On the bridge, First Officer William Murdoch, told the helmsman, Robert Hitchens, to turn *Titanic* hard to port (left), and ordered the engineers to put the ship into reverse.

THE ICEBERG STRIKES

Titanic slowly turned, but only enough to avoid a head-on collision. After an agonising wait of 37 seconds, *Titanic* smashed into the iceberg along her starboard (right) side.

The ship's telegraph was used to tell the engineers below decks to change speed or reverse the ship.

Slowly Sinking

As her forward compartments filled with water, *Titanic* slowly sank from the bows. On the bridge, Fourth Officer Boxhall fired distress rockets, hoping that they would be seen by another ship.

LOADING THE LIFEBOATS

The crew helped people onto lifeboats, until the last two boats were launched by floating them straight off the sinking ship. After all the lifeboats had gone, more than 1,500 people remained on board *Titanic*.

LEFT ON BOARD

Most of those who remained on the ship made their way to the rising stern, clinging to deck fittings and railings. As the deck grew too steep to stand on, some jumped into the icy sea, hoping to swim to a lifeboat. Even at this late stage, the ship's lights continued to shine, thanks to the engineers, who bravely remained at their posts.

Boat Deck: The Wheelhouse
You are standing in the wheelhouse of Titanic, where the helmsman steered the ship using the wheel. The room in front is the bridge, where the officer in charge of navigating the ship kept watch and gave orders.

"*An iceberg, sir. I hard-a-starboarded and reversed the engines and I was going to hard-a-port around it, but she was too close.*" **First Officer, William Murdoch.**

FIRST OFFICER WILLIAM MURDOCH

ABANDON SHIP!

Shortly after the collision with the iceberg, Captain Smith and Thomas Andrews, *Titanic*'s builder, inspected the damage. Andrews told the captain that the ship was doomed and would sink in just two hours.

This iceberg, photographed in the Atlantic on 12 April, may be the one that *Titanic* struck.

ICE DAMAGE
The iceberg opened a 90m gash along the ship's starboard side, flooding six of her watertight compartments. These were only watertight to a limited height. Once water reached the top of each compartment, it would spill over into the next one. Eventually, the ship would sink.

LIFEJACKETS
Soon after midnight, Captain Smith gave orders to prepare to abandon ship. The crew, summoned by alarm bells, uncovered the lifeboats and handed out lifejackets. There was a lifejacket for everyone on the ship. A lifejacket would keep its wearer afloat, but it gave no protection from the deadly cold of the icy sea.

Titanic's lifejackets were made from cork floats covered with canvas fabric.

TITANIC SINKING

You are looking at the sinking Titanic from one of her lifeboats. It is about 2am and the ship's lights are still shining, but in just twenty minutes she would be gone.

SS CALIFORNIAN

Just a few kilometres away, another ship, SS *Californian*, had stopped for the night in an ice field. The officers on duty saw the lights of *Titanic* and the rockets she fired, but they did not realize that the ship was sinking. Unfortunately, *Californian*'s radio operator had gone to bed, so the ship never received *Titanic*'s distress message.

LAUNCH THE LIFEBOATS

Smith ordered his officers to fill the lifeboats. Women and children were to be the first to board them. *Titanic* had 20 lifeboats, enough to carry just 1,178 of the 2,223 people on board. The only hope for passengers unable to find a place in a lifeboat was that rescuers would arrive before the ship sank.

On the Boat Deck there were 14 large wooden lifeboats. Each boat could hold 65 people.

This is the only photograph of a radio operator at work on *Titanic*. Radio messages could be received up to 1,600km away.

SEND HELP!

At 12.10am, Smith ordered the ship's radio operators to send out distress calls. Using Morse code, in which short and long signals stand for letters, the operators called for help. They sent the traditional distress signal, CQD, as well as a recently introduced new signal, SOS.

"We are sinking fast. Passengers are being put into boats."

Last message sent by radio operator, Jack Phillips.

JACK PHILLIPS

TO THE LIFEBOATS

Panic and confusion grew as news of the emergency spread and the lifeboats were lowered. There had been no lifeboat drill, so many of the passengers and crew didn't know what to do.

WOMEN AND CHILDREN FIRST

Officers Murdoch and Lightoller were in charge of the lifeboats on each side of the ship. They filled them with women and children first, plus a few crewmen to pull the oars. Many women did not want to leave their husbands behind and some lifeboats left the ship half-empty.

The lifeboats had to be slowly lowered from a height of 18m to the sea below.

THE LAST BOATS

As it became clear that the ship was really sinking, there was a scramble for places in the lifeboats. By the time the third-class passengers managed to find their way to the top deck, almost all of the lifeboats had gone.

This artist's impression shows the lifeboats being filled in an orderly way, with women saying goodbye to the men, who stand back.

"There weren't enough boats to take half the people and the chances of the other half in that icy cold water were absolutely nil."

Second Officer, Charles Lightoller.

CHARLES LIGHTOLLER

CHARLES HENDRICKSON

> *"It's up to us to go back and pick up anyone in the water."*
>
> **Crewman Charles Hendrickson, on Lifeboat 1.**

THE LAST VIEW

Fearing being sucked under by the sinking ship, the lifeboat crews rowed as far away as possible. At 2.20am, they watched as *Titanic* finally disappeared beneath the water. With the ship gone, the air was filled with cries for help from hundreds of people in the water.

Lifeboat 14, towing one of the canvas collapsible lifeboats, photographed on the morning after the sinking.

Messrs Coutts Bank Ltd. April 16
Strand. London. W.C.

Pay to J. Hoswell, or order.
The Sum of Five Pounds.

£5 . 0 . 0.   Cosmo Duff Gordon

Sir Cosmo Duff Gordon instructed his bank to pay each of the crewmen in his lifeboat.

NO GOING BACK

In different lifeboats, Molly Brown, Charles Hendrickson and Lady Rothes each suggested returning to pick up survivors. They were overruled by passengers who thought the boats would be swamped. One lady said, 'Why should we all lose our lives in a useless attempt to save others from the ship?'

LIFEBOAT FOR HIRE?

Lifeboat Number 1 could have gone back for more survivors. It was built to hold 40 people, but carried only twelve, including Sir Cosmo and Lady Duff Gordon. Sir Cosmo later gave money to the crewmen and was accused of hiring his own personal lifeboat.

MOLLY BROWN

THE COUNTESS OF ROTHES

A Deck: Grand Central Staircase

You are looking down at the Titanic's Grand Central Staircase, as the waters rise, step by step. In a few moments, the lights will go out, and water from the deck above will smash through the glass dome over the staircase and into the ship.

LAST MOMENTS

Survivors later gave accounts of the bravery of those who went down with *Titanic*. Among those celebrated as heroes were the ship's musicians, who played as the ship sank, and the US millionaire Benjamin Guggenheim.

BENJAMIN GUGGENHEIM

LIKE GENTLEMEN

Guggenheim made no effort to save himself and even refused to wear a lifejacket. After helping to load the lifeboats, he returned to his cabin with his valet, where they put on full evening dress, to await their fate 'like gentlemen'.

To the end, *Titanic's* musicians played lively tunes, to keep up the passengers' spirits.

> "We've dressed up in our best and are prepared to go down like gentlemen."
>
> **Benjamin Guggenheim, speaking to a steward.**

THE ILLUSTRATED LONDON NEWS, APRIL 27, 1912.—638

BRAVE AS THE "BIRKENHEAD" BAND: THE "TITANIC'S" MUSICIAN HEROES.

THE RESCUE

Although many ships received *Titanic*'s radio distress calls, only one was close enough to help. This was the Cunard liner, RMS *Carpathia*, commanded by Captain Arthur Rostron.

MESSAGE RECEIVED

When she received the distress call at 12.25 am, *Carpathia* was about 93 kilometres southeast of *Titanic* and heading east. Captain Rostron immediately gave orders to change course. He prepared his ship in every detail, ordering hot drinks, soup and medical supplies to be prepared, and cabins made ready for the survivors.

Carpathia was on her way from New York to Gibralta when the distress call came from *Titanic*.

MAXIMUM SPEED

Carpathia was supposed to have a maximum speed of 14 knots (26km/hr). However, by setting every stoker to work, Rostron boosted the ship's speed to over 17 knots (31km/h). Unaccustomed to this power, the ship's decks shook as she steamed towards *Titanic*.

CAPTAIN
ARTHUR ROSTRON

"*Icebergs loomed up and fell astern; we never slackened, though sometimes we altered course suddenly to avoid them.*"

Captain Arthur Rostron, recalling the race to reach *Titanic*.

PRESENTED
TO THE
CAPTAIN
OFFICERS & CREW
OF
R.M.S. "CARPATHIA"
IN RECOGNITION OF GALLANT &
HEROIC SERVICES
FROM THE SURVIVORS
OF THE
S.S. "TITANIC"
APRIL 15TH 1912

DIEGES & CLUST
N.Y.

The grateful survivors from *Titanic*
later presented 320 medals to the crew
of *Carpathia*.

THE RESCUE BEGINS

Carpathia reached the scene of the disaster at 4am,
an hour and 45 minutes after *Titanic* had sunk.
By now, the lifeboats were scattered over several
square kilometres of sea. It took four hours for the
rescuers to pick up all 706 survivors.

Huddled on the deck of *Carpathia*, the
survivors are wrapped in blankets.

SILENT SURVIVORS

Captain Rostron was struck by how quiet the survivors
were. There was no celebration at being rescued. Many
women had lost husbands and were suffering from
shock and grief. Children who had lost their fathers
still hoped that by some miracle they might be found.

THE DEAD

The rescuers arrived too late for the passengers in the
water, who all died in their first hour in the icy sea.
Over the next few days, other ships would arrive to
search for the dead. In all, 337 bodies were retrieved;
128 of them were buried at sea.

Survivors from Lifeboat 1, safely
aboard *Carpathia*, including Sir Cosmo
Duff Gordon (back row, third from left).

After the Tragedy

News that *Titanic* had sunk quickly spread around the world. Everywhere, people were shocked and fascinated by the disaster. Within months, the first films, songs and books about *Titanic* appeared.

NEWS OF THE DISASTER
For weeks, news of the *Titanic* disaster and the loss of 1,517 lives filled the papers. Many stories were told of the heroic self-sacrifice of the crew and the male passengers who died. A myth also developed that *Titanic*'s builders had claimed she was 'unsinkable'.

LESSONS LEARNED
In New York and London, there were inquiries into why the disaster had happened. Both concluded that *Titanic* was travelling too fast and recommended new safety regulations. Ships would now have to carry enough lifeboats for everybody on board.

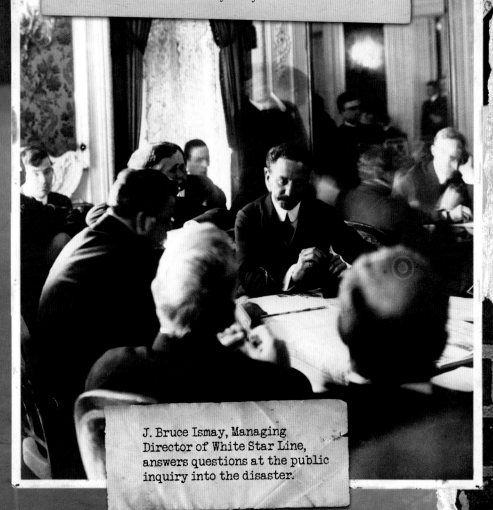

J. Bruce Ismay, Managing Director of White Star Line, answers questions at the public inquiry into the disaster.

A newspaper boy outside the White Star Line's office in London, on 16 April 1912.

REMEMBERING *TITANIC*

The loss of *Titanic* was felt most deeply in Southampton, home to 724 members of the crew, of whom only 175 survived. In 1914, more than 100,000 gathered here for the unveiling of a memorial to *Titanic*'s engineers.

The Southampton Memorial to the engineers on board *Titanic*, who died at their posts.

" 'Be British' was the cry as the ship went down
Every man was steady at his post
Captain and crew when they knew the worst
Saving the women and children first."

Lyrics to 'Be British' by Lawrence Wright, 1912.

UNFORGETTABLE!
BREATHTAKING!
BRILLIANT!

TOLD AS IT REALLY HAPPENED!

A NIGHT TO REMEMBER

A NEW MOTION PICTURE
Never before seen on
Screen or
Television!

The screenplay of *A Night to Remember* was based on interviews with survivors.

NOTHING ON EARTH
COULD COME BETWEEN THEM.

LEONARDO DiCAPRIO KATE WINSLET

TITANIC

Titanic used the disaster as the setting for a love story between passengers from different classes.

THE RANK ORGANIZATION presents
KENNETH MORE in
A NIGHT TO REMEMBER
Based on the book by WALTER LORD

BE BRITISH!

Captain Smith, who died on *Titanic*, was declared a hero. According to one newspaper, Smith's last words, shouted through a megaphone, were 'Be British!' This story inspired a popular song, released on record in 1912 to raise money for survivors.

TITANIC MOVIES

There have been more than twenty movies about *Titanic*, the first two released within months of the sinking. The most historically accurate is *A Night to Remember* (1958). The best known is *Titanic* (1997), one of the most successful movies ever.

TITANIC TODAY

Titanic still lies 3,800m down, on the Atlantic seabed, where she sank a century ago. The wreck was discovered in 1985, by a joint French and US expedition led by Dr. Robert Ballard.

DISCOVERY

Ballard found the wreck after a two-month search using an unmanned mini-submarine. *Titanic* had split in two, with her bow and stern sections settling 600m apart. Between them, debris from the ship lay scattered across the seabed.

The rusting bow of *Titanic* on the seabed, its railings still in place.

The bronze starboard propeller is perfectly preserved. Unlike iron, bronze does not rust.

China dishes stacked up in neat rows where they landed on the seabed.

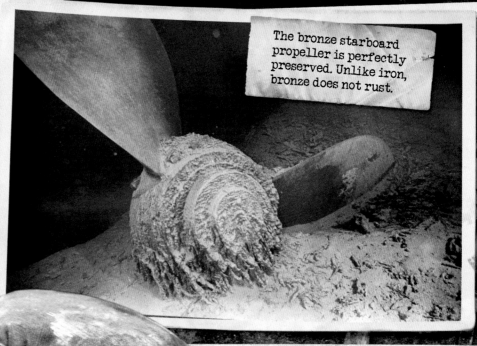

RELICS

Ballard believed that the wreck should be left untouched. However, in the 1990s, a US company called RMS *Titanic,* Inc. began to salvage objects from the ship. Since then, more than 5,500 artefacts have been recovered and put on display in a series of travelling exhibitions.

This battered silk top hat belonged to one of the first-class passengers.

THE FUTURE OF *TITANIC*?

The wreck of *Titanic* is gradually collapsing, as the wrought iron of the ship is eaten away by metal-eating microbes. Nobody is quite sure how long the actual ship will survive, but our fascination with the most famous ship in history shows no signs of fading away. *Titanic* will never be forgotten.

Fig. 1.

Fig. 2. PROMENADE DECK (A)

ELEC. CRANE

VERANDAH AND PALM COURT

1ST CLASS

1ST CLASS

CLOAK ROOM

ENGINE UPTAKE CASING

BOILER UPTAKE CASING

COMPANION

SMOKE ROOM CASING

WELL

ENTRANCE

TANK ROOM

LOUNGE D° PANTRY

LOUNGE BAR

VERANDAH AND PALM COURT

SMOKE ROOM

ELEC. CRANE

1ST CL. PROMENADE

Fig. 3.

BRIDGE DECK (B)

POOP DECK.

ELEC. CRANE

ELEC. CRANE

2ND CLASS PROMENADE

1ST CLASS PROMENADE

FIN

CAPSTAN

CAPSTAN

SKYLIGHT

ELEC. WINCH

Nº4 HATCH

SMOKE ROOM BAR

2ND CLASS ENTRANCE

2ND CLASS SMOKE ROOM

WELL

2ND CLASS

RESTAURANT

PANTRY

SCULLERY & GALLEY

TURBINE ENGINE ROOM CASING

WELL

UP

ENGINE ROOM CASING

BOILER UPTAKE CASING

BATH

BATH

FAN

CAPSTAN

SKYLIGHT

ELEC. CRANE

UP

ENTRANCE

SMOKE ROOM LAVY

Nº4 HATCH

WINE ROOM

UP

WELL

BATH

BATH

CAPSTAN

ELEC. CRANE

SUITE OF ROOMS

SUITE